MAPMAKERS AND THE LOST MAGIC

Mapmakers and the Lost Magic was written with pencil and paper before being transferred to a Word document. It was drawn and colored digitally in Photoshop and lettered with the artist's own handwritten font.

Visit us on the web! RHKidsGraphic.com • @RHKidsGraphic

Educators and librarians, for a variety of teaching tools, visit us at RHTeachersLibrarians.com

Library of Congress Cataloging-in-Publication Data is available upon request.
ISBN 978-0-593-17287-2 (hardcover) — ISBN 978-0-593-17286-5 (paperback)
ISBN 978-0-593-17289-6 (ebook) — ISBN 978-0-593-17288-9 (lib. bdg.)

Designed by Patrick Crotty
Title design by Walter Parenton

MANUFACTURED IN CHINA
10 9 8 7 6 5 4 3 2 1
First Edition

A comic on every bookshelf.

Mapmakers and the Lost Magic

Written by

CAMERON CHITTOCK

Illustrated by

AMANDA CASTILLO

For Tay
—C.C.

Para mi abuelo. Te quiero por siempre.
Este es mi adiós para ti.
—A.C.

We're lost,
Alidade.

We're not lost, Lewis. This is just the scenic route.

Uh huh.

One day we'll go somewhere without any **detours**.
Oh, come on . . .

Where's the fun in that?

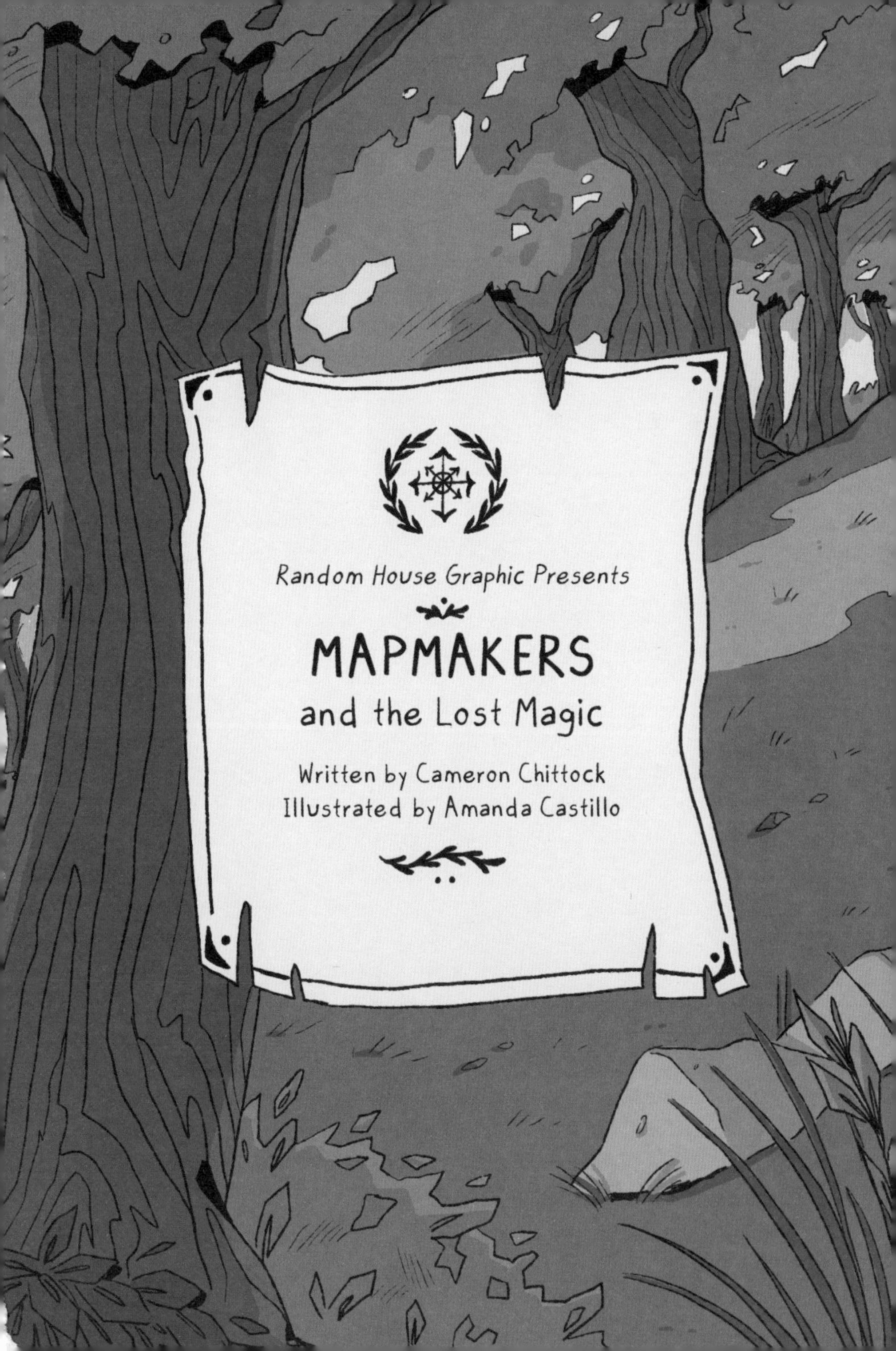
Random House Graphic Presents
MAPMAKERS
and the Lost Magic
Written by Cameron Chittock
Illustrated by Amanda Castillo

Right here. This is where I wanted to be.
You, me . . .

. . . and this view.
Uh . . . Alidade?

That's just home.

Wrong direction. Not **Alden** . . .

Out **there**. The horizon. Where anything is possible.

It's nothing but **clouds**. Big gray clouds, all year round.

You really want to leave Alden one day, don't you?

Leave behind the same little town I've known my whole life?
Yeah. I really do.

Out there?
I read there are **mountains** completely untouched by mankind.
And **plains** where pheasants herd in the thousands.
How are you going to find all that if you still get lost in our dinky little forest?
Hey, I got us here! Eventually . . .
HA
HA
HA!
RSSSt
RSSt

What was that?!
RSST
RSSST

Maybe it was just a squirrel or something.

Yeah, maybe.
RSSST
RSST

Or worse . . .

Night Coats.
You two again.
RUN!

HEY!

This way!
Fleeing the scene only makes things worse!

We can lose them if we just—

—Alidade?!
Alidade, where'd you go?!

Why do you always get lost at the **worst** times . . .

LEWIS?!
Ugh.

What the . . .

?

A doorknob?

There you are! Thank goodness. Come on, we gotta keep moving!

But—

Al!
It was right here—

THERE YOU ARE!

Watch where you're going, Lewis!
Sorry, Mr. Bradley! Excuse us, Ms. Irving! I'll make it up to you!

Pshh.
At least we know he means it.

Move it!
OOF

Al . . . we can't outrun them forever.
Don't worry . . .

. . . we'll lose 'em at the **brick pit.**

Lewis? You shouldn't be here, m'boy.
Sorry, Mr. Ford—we're looking to change that right away. Promise.

HUFF HUFF
HUFF HUFF

Last warning, you two!

You know the **rules**!
Alidade . . .

You were out past the town's limits.

You can't just go wherever you want!
Watch me.

Okay. We can do this. Up onto the log bridge and into the clear.
You and me . . .
No matter what.
GO!

!

Miss Rose
and Mr. Briar.
Lost again?
I'm sure
I can help you
find your way.

We can manage . . . Madam Constable.

Why so formal? No need to pretend you respect our authority now.

I take it you enjoyed the view from on the hill? Always good to put things in perspective . . .

. . . and remember just how much of your world belongs to me.

All this? You can have it. And one day—
ROLL

—ah!

One day you'll learn you prefer the view from **down here**.

There's only one place capable of such . . . creative craftsmanship.

"Let's go pay your mother a visit, Miss Rose."

I would, Mrs. Rose, if that's all right?

Constable Atwater. What a nice surprise. You've never been one for quilting.

No, a bit below my taste I'm afraid. But—

I did want to bring forward something we **do** have a shared interest in.

Alidade!
Lewis??

They were outside Alden's boundary.

And that was before they made a **scene** in the brick pit.

Terrorizing the people working to keep this town afloat.
That's not true—

Alidade! Not another word.

Their mishap provides an opportunity to remind **everyone** what the Night Coats expect from the people of Alden.

Obedience. And nothing less.

Since you two are so fond of the pit, I'm sure you'd relish the chance to spend the summer cleaning it up. What do you say?
Yes, Madam Constable.

Lovely. See you tomorrow.
Enjoy the rest of your meeting, everyone . . .

. . . I can't wait to see the results of all your hard work.

We're going to pay for that.

It might be a **game** to your kid, but not us.
The Night Coats will punish **the whole town** if they need to.
Not if we keep our heads down. This was just a warning.

Let's hope so. They're not ones for mercy.

I think that's enough excitement for one evening.
And people say quilt-making is **boring**. Heh.

Weren't **you** supposed to be watching Lewis?
He was right with the others! Or, uh, I **thought** he was . . .

Ma—
You're filthy.

Ma, I'm sorry, but we weren't—

Where you were supposed to be? I **hope** that's what you're getting at.

No, I just—ugh. It's not **fair**.

Do you think it'd be **fair** if your neighbors were punished for something **you** did?
Because **next time**, there will be consequences for **all** of us.

You spend too much time thinking of the world "out there," Alidade.
You've got to keep your head down. That's the Alden way.

You should have been here quilting like a member of the community.
Well, maybe I don't want to be part of this community

Excuse me, young lady?

What?! What's so bad about wanting to see more than this stupid town?
Our family has called this "stupid town" home for **generations**.
And look how good that's worked out!

Not much of a **family** when we're the **only two** left.

Okay, Alidade. You may be excused.

Ma, I—
Go.

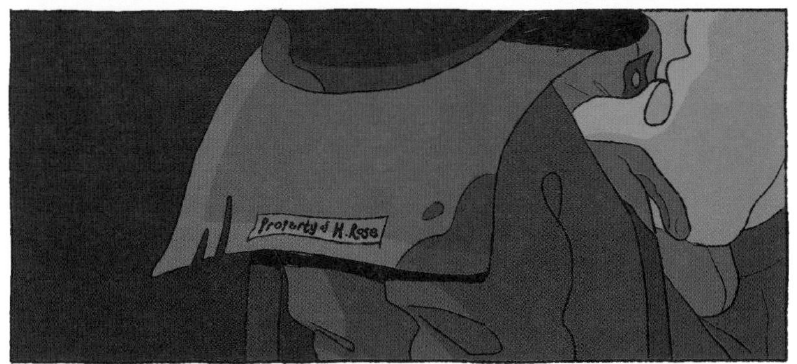
Property of H. Rose

Sorry, Ma.

Where—
huff
—**are** you? I swear you were right here.

AHH!
SSKKKRTT

WHHHSSSSHHH

It's just the **woods.** Nothing strange in the woods—

Nothing strange at all . . .

Ugh.
Lewis can never know about this.

?
RMMMMMMBBB

SKRRSSH
GAHH!
SKRRSH

Not good.

Come on,
come on—
SMACK!
OOF
What in the stars was that?!
Glass?
Since when was there glass—

—here.
Oh.

Wherever "here" is.

Just so you know . . . this is **not** trespassing! **You** invited me.
A magic doorknob is close enough to an invitation, anyway.

Hellooooo!
. . .

Huh.

All these logs and there's only **one** that's loose?

I wonder what makes **you** special.

coff coff
Blech!

Whoa . . .

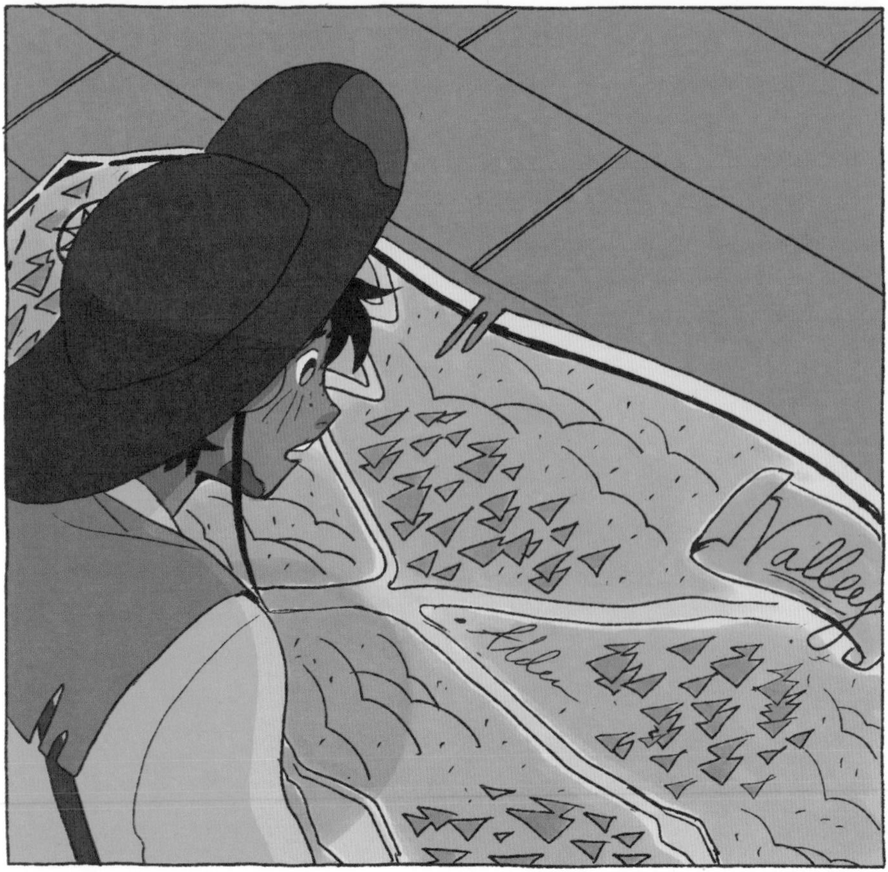

It's beautiful.
Valley

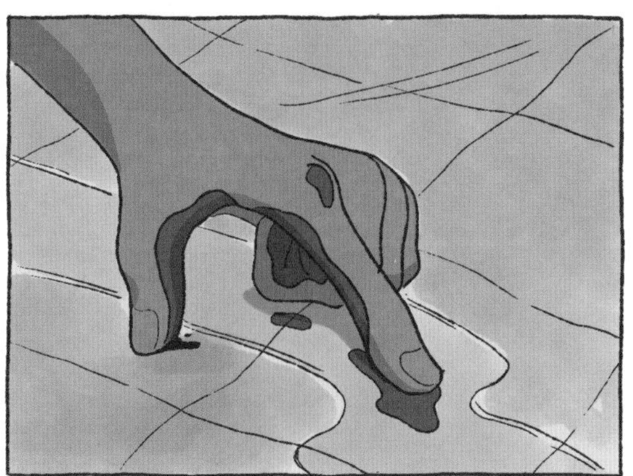

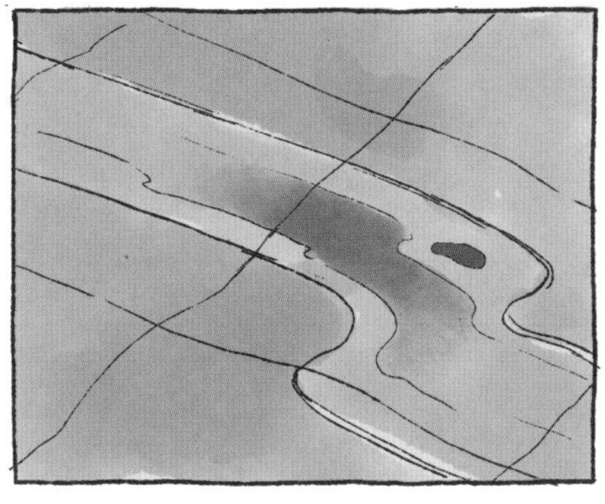

Wait—

Alden
Alden?

What are you doing here?

Alden

That doesn't look right . . .

Hey!

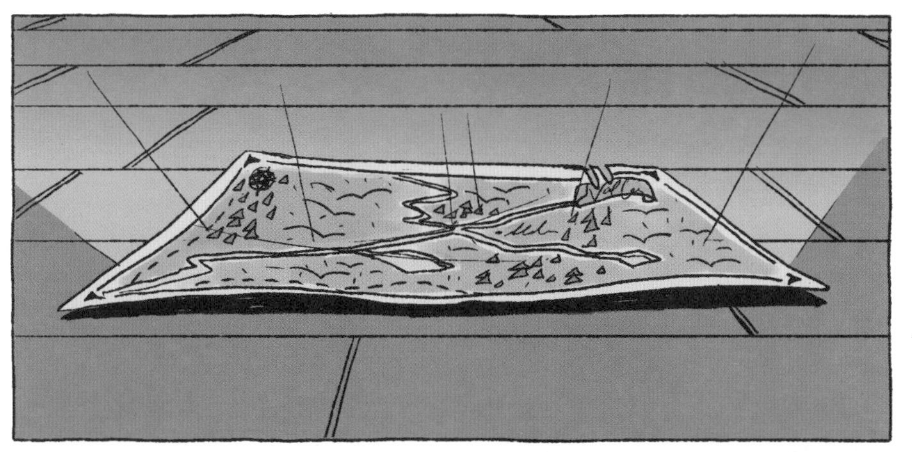

Valley

What—
How—
Where'd **you** come from?

?
?

GAHH!
AHHH!

What are you?
Who are you?!

You can talk?!

Wait—did you say "what are you"?
You think I'm a "what"? A "thing"?

Hn. Humans.

Disrespectful, arrogant, and . . . well, you are clearly dealing with some hygiene issues.
Hygiene issues?! What do you know? You're just a . . . a . . . what is even happening right now?!

Okay, okay. Deep breaths.
My name is Alidade. Alidade Rose. And . . . and you are?

Oh, me? Why, I am—

—tiny?! Why am I so tiny? I look like a pigeon. It's a disgrace!

My map—
where is my
map?

Oh, uh . . .
here. Over
here.

I found
it. In—in
the wall.
Hm.

Forgotten.

KAFF
KAFF

Are you okay??
Did that **sound** okay?!
What can I do? I've got all kinds of stuff in my satchel . . .

No. I know what happens when people like **you** try to help . . .

People like **me**?
Yes. **People.** You are a person, are you not?

Hey, I'm the one who got you out of this map thing!

Precisely! Just the kind of stupid thing a person would do.

Wait. You **wanted** to be stuck in there?
I don't belong out here. Not anymore.

Why . . . why is **my town** on this map? I've never seen any of these places before.
What do you mean you've never—

—what's happened to the Valley, Alidade Rose?

Where are the **Mapmakers**?

I—I—

WHERE ARE THEY?

Wait—!

That . . . that was . . .

Awesome.

KNOK
KNOK
KNOK

Lewis!! Come on, we gotta go!
KNOK KNOK KNOK

How can you **possibly** be this excited?

We're cleaning a big ol' pile of dirt with the Constable—and we're gonna be late!

You're saying bad things . . . but **smiling.** It's terrifying.

Alidade . . . what aren't you telling me? You know I hate surprises.
No surprises! The sooner we get started . . .

". . . the sooner
we're free."

You were right. No surprises—this **is** the worst.

We're almost done.
Almost done?!

You Aldeners never change. Always looking for the easy way out.

Judging by the look of the pit . . .
. . . I'd say you're just getting started.

Get comfy. It's the job you'll have for the rest of your life. Along with the rest of your fellow townies.

And we're happy to do it, Night Coats, sirs. We're on it.

All right. That's enough for today.

Oh, thank the stars.

Be here **on time** tomorrow.

Okay that sounds lovely thanks so much can't wait byyye!

They're still a bit—
Unruly? Yeah . . .

". . . we'll need to clean that up, too."

ALIDADE! SLOW. DOWN.

My back hurts. My legs hurt. My arms . . . hurt. Everything **hurts**.
But we're back in the same woods that got us into this mess.

It's the source of the **hurting**. Why are you taking me here?

Because! It's the source of much **more** than that.

Okay, in we go. You first.
. . .
A door in a tree? **That's why** we're here?

Is—is this a joke to you?
We're in trouble, Al. Not with our parents or some bullies— the **Night Coats.**

This isn't time for one of your . . . **pretend adventures!**

I know this is my fault, but just . . . trust me. Okay?

Yeah. Fine.
No matter what.

But after this, I'm going to lie down. For like . . . ever.

Why don't you get lost like **this** more often?! This is AMAZING!

And you just . . . found the doorknob?

When we were running from the Night Coats and got separated, it . . . appeared. Like magic.

This place has all sorts of magic.
And it's like they say in books—the best magic . . .

. . . requires a little . . .

. . . more . . .

. . . work.

This thing is
old. The clay's not
going to mess
it up?

Without it,
it's just an old
map. But with
it . . .

You've
returned. How
disappointing.

You brought
someone?!
No one should
know I exist!
Uh . . . I'm
Lewis.

Okay, child, let it out. Get the oohing and ahhing out of the way.

. . . how are you so **small**?
YOU **DARE** INSULT ME?!

I'm sorry, Mr.—wait, you never told me your name.
And I do not intend to!

Hey! I have so many questions. I still don't know what—I mean, **who**—you **are**!

I'm someone who wants to be left **alone**!

I do not know that I **have** answers to your questions. I have been gone a long time.
Long enough that the world may have passed me by.

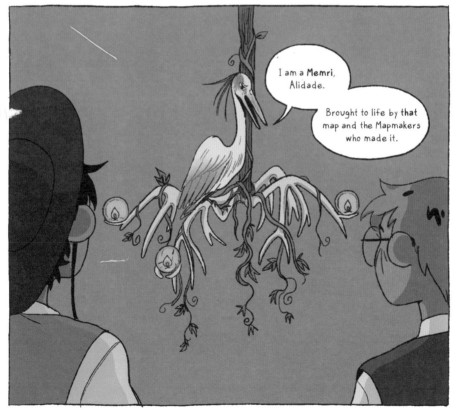

I am a **Memri**, Alidade.

Brought to life by **that** map and the Mapmakers who made it.

. . . you're a what, now?
You've never heard of the Memris?!
"Mapmakers bring us to life so we might guide humanity to live in harmony with the natural world.
"We are protectors of the land and peace."
Or . . . we **used** to be.

Was this place . . . your home?
It's the **Mapmakers' Lodge.** A . . . waystation for the Mapmakers, those who sought to better understand the world and share that knowledge with others.

That's a fancy way of saying they helped people get from Point A to Point B . . .

Boy, there is more power and wisdom in a Mapmaker's map than you can **imagine**!

Memris are proof of that.

But, Mr. Blue, sir, um — if you're proof of all this power, how come you're so tiny?

I think what Lewis means is . . . **something** happened to you. Right?

Yes. If I am this weak, it's because my map no longer reflects the land. It must have . . . **changed**.

I imagine we have the Night Coats to thank for that.
He knows about the Night Coats?

Oh yes, very well.

But . . . how could the Night Coats have done this?
The way people have always divided one another: lies and power.

"Despite the Memris' best efforts, there were disputes among the territories.
"When it looked like war was on the horizon, the Night Coats rose up, promising to maintain order.

"They hid their true plan: to eliminate the Memris and rule alone."

The last thing I remember was my fellow Memris trying to stop it, but . . . clearly, we were too late.

To be whole again . . . you'd need a Mapmaker to update your map. So . . . maybe you can teach **me**.

And why would you want to do that?
Yeah. My question exactly.

I don't know. They must . . . **travel** and see the world, right? And—and help people!
Why wouldn't someone want to do that?

Child. Will you look around?

The way of the Mapmakers is not the fantastic life you're imagining.

It's a life in **ruins**.

The Night Coats are still in power. The Mapmakers **failed**.

Only **people** are capable of creating an end so bleak.

The best thing for you to do is forget this ever happened.
Maybe he's right, Al.

Maybe it's time to head back.

People saved your life!

What?
Your map. It wasn't . . . forgotten. It was **hidden**. By people.

When everything went wrong, **someone** didn't give up. And I won't, either.
If your map needs to be fixed . . . I can help.

Are you sure about this?
He needs us, Lewis.

Okay, I'm in. **Someone's** gotta make sure you don't get lost.

Hm. Okay, Alidade Rose. I will teach you how to be a Mapmaker.

But if you give me one reason to think this is a mistake, that's the end of it.

Now . . . it's time to see what happened to my Valley.

You're **sure** you saw them come up here, Tace?
One hundred percent, Ada. They left the pit and headed back this way.

To the same place we caught them last time. Heh.
Maybe the Constable **will** be able to make an example of them.

That's the plan.

WE KNOW YOU'RE OUT HERE!

Make this easy on yourselves and come back with us!
Willingly!
Uh . . . not good.

Can they see us?
Not while we're inside the lodge.
What do we do?

I suppose it's time you saw what "Point A to Point B" looks like.

Over there! You hear that?
SNAP!

Here we are—pick one!

Gotchya.
SHHK
SHHK

"One hundred percent," huh?
At least we know they're not up to anything.

I don't think I liked that.
hic
Yup. Didn't like that.

Where are we?
Where you have always been: the Valley.
Wait . . .
WHERE IS THE RIVER?!

The what?

Our **river**! All that time with my map and you failed to notice the giant blue streak?

Well . . . there's no river here.
Don't think there's ever been one.

Oh, there was. And it . . .
. . . it was **everything**.

No wonder I'm so weak. If the river dried up . . . we have more work to do than I realized.

We had better get started.
Aren't we going to need more clay?

No, we will need something far more permanent.

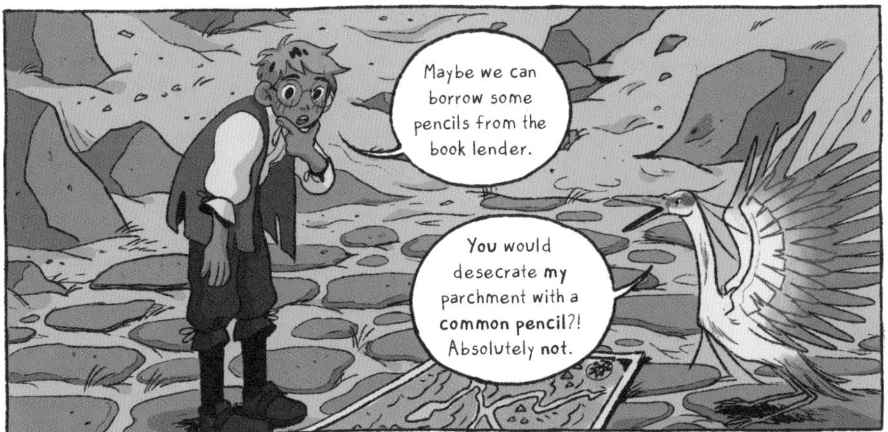
Maybe we can borrow some pencils from the book lender.
You would desecrate **my** parchment with a **common pencil**?! Absolutely **not**.

We are not merely drawing a picture. We are casting a spell.

A lot of things must go right for a spell to work. For mapmaking, there are three tenets.

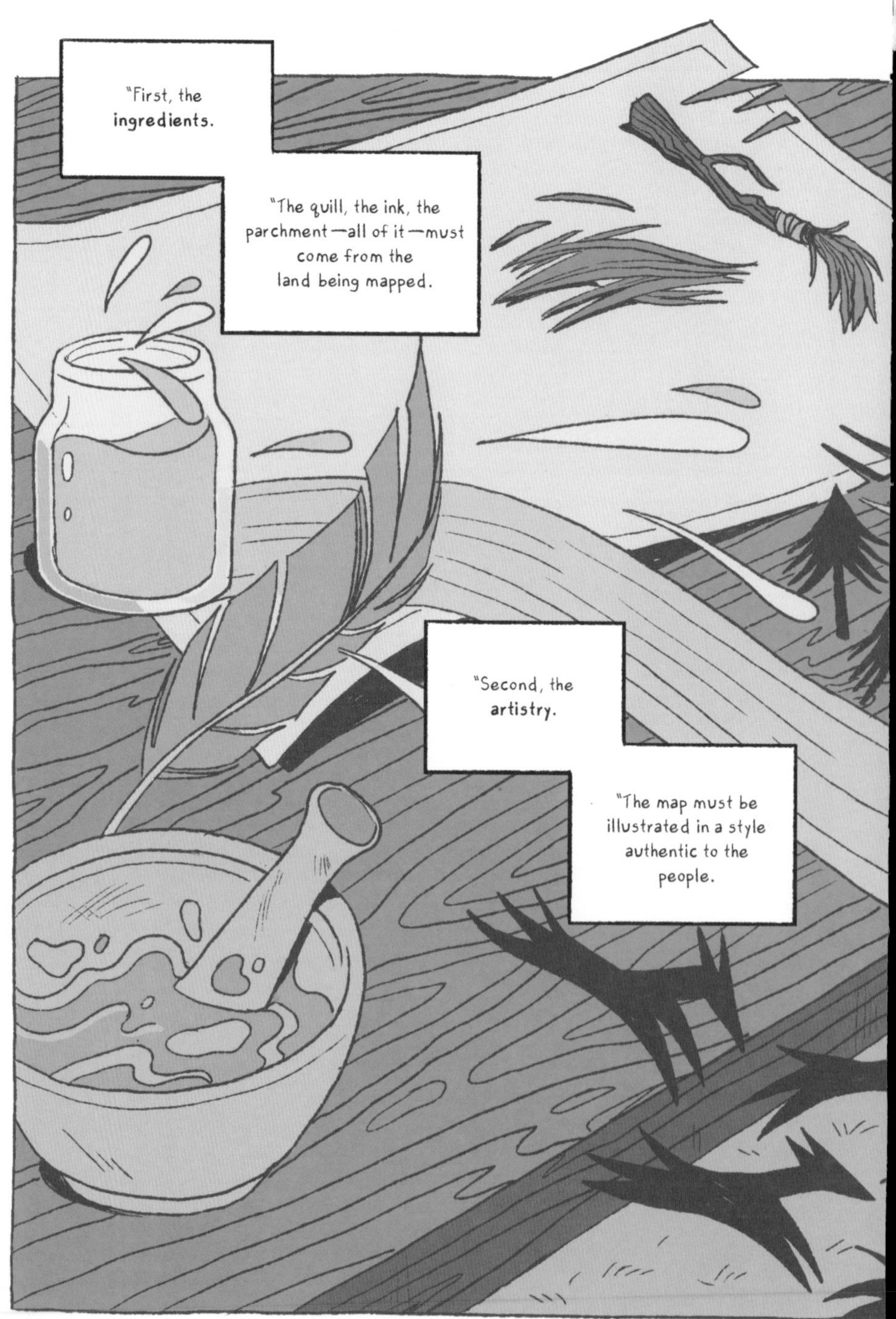
"First, the **ingredients**.
"The quill, the ink, the parchment—all of it—must come from the land being mapped.
"Second, the **artistry**.
"The map must be illustrated in a style authentic to the people.

"And finally, the **accuracy**.
"The map must properly convey its land down to the detail."

If any **one** of the tenets is not precise, the map is useless.

Once completed, a Mapmaker adds their signature to bind it all together: the **compass rose**.

I can teach you, but **you** will have to reintroduce me to the land. I . . . do not recognize it.
That's okay, we know it pretty well.

Now, to prove you can be in tune with the world around you, you must find your **first ingredient**.

"I suggest you start your search at the Tree with a Broken Heart.
"An old tree and a dear friend, so please be on your best behavior.

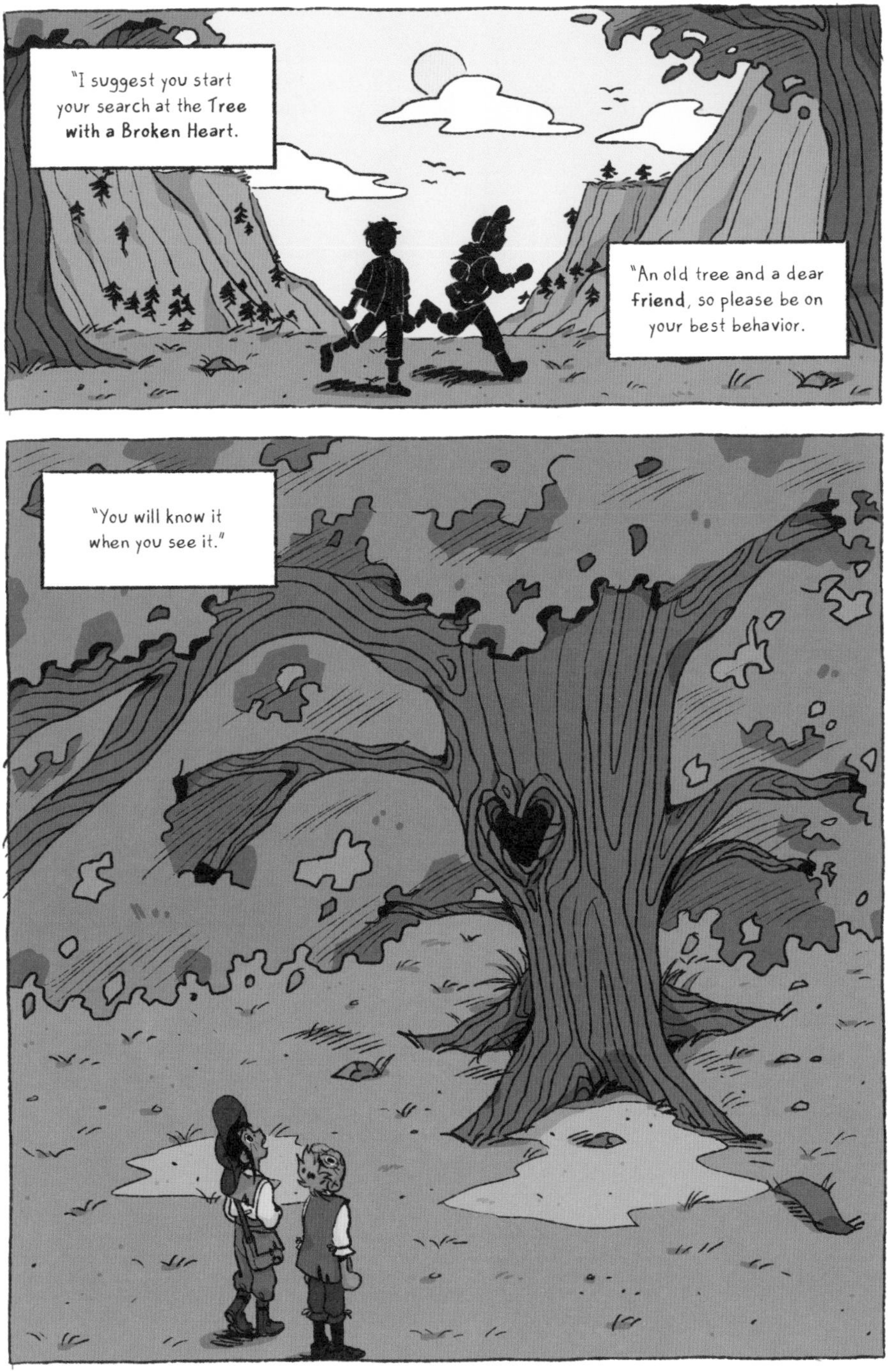

"You will know it when you see it."

Keep your eye out for something special.

Uh—these yellow-tailed ravens look more . . . **hungry** than special.
SQWAK!

They're **birds**. They're not going to **eat** you.

But I think I found what they **do** eat . . .

. . . a lightning worm hive!

They're kinda cute. In their own . . . gross way. What do we do with them?

We smash 'em.
WHAT?!

What do you mean "smash 'em"?!
You saw the colors on Blue's map! They're faded now, but they must have been **bright** back in the day.

Look at the glow of the worms— it **must** be for making ink!
The first ingredient is dead-worm ink?

I won't let you murder them.

Murder? They're just **worms**. I've seen you **eat** worms!
I was five! And it was **one time**.

What am I supposed to do? This is part of my training.
Or it's a test.
Same thing!

Oh no, tests are different. Tests mean he's trying to **stump** you, not teach you.

Lewis, if I'm going to be a Mapmaker I've got to be adventurous!
SQWAK!
See—the yellow-tail understands!

I'm in tune with nature already.
MURDERER!

You . . . you just . . . **smashed** them?!

I thought they were the first ingredient.
Oh, I'm sure **you** did!

Destruction is always the first ingredient for humans, isn't it?
You followed your instinct and **that** is where it led you!

I knew I should have let this all be.
You are no different!

Wait, where are you going? I'm sorry, okay!
Back to the lodge. No murderers allowed.

I was wrong. It appears **little** has changed.

SLAM
Lewis, you were right about the worms.

And . . .
You were right about it being a test.

Told you. But hey. Tomorrow's another day to try and pass . . .

". . . at least you know it can't go any worse!"

SPLLT
Hey, you missed something!

That's the **worst** clean-upsmanship I've ever seen.
I wonder where **this** came from . . .

What was that?! Speak up, son.
And choose your next words carefully.

I'd give the same advice to you two.

M-Madam Constable, sir! What a surprise. We were just—
Private Tace. Private Ada. You're **dismissed**. And please do not rush back.

I apologize. This work is supposed to be hard enough on its own, without . . . fanfare.
How are you two holding up?

. . .

I'm going to work where the only pests are the mosquitoes.

She is stubborn, isn't she?
Like you wouldn't believe.

Not the first stubborn person from these parts, though.
What do **you** know about it?

Mr. Briar, where do you think I'm **from**?

Oh yes, Alden through and through. That's why my boss picked me to oversee this region.

I spent many summers cleaning up this **awful** patch.
Really?

I know this seems like the end of the world. I used to **rage** against it.
But the bricks are our livelihood.

Before you or I were born . . . Alden was desperate for work. People went hungry. It was a dire time for our town.

The **Night Coats** showed our people how to make the bricks and turn this pit into something useful: a second chance.

It's grueling work, but it's tradition for everyone to chip in.

Do you want to know the trick to getting through it?

Keep your head down.
Keep your head down and before you know it . . .

. . . you'll forget about the fantasies you were chasing.

They pull us away from where we belong.

In my experience . . .

"...fantasies only tear us apart."
SMAK

Gah, I'm sorry, mosquito!!
Ugh. First the worms, now you.

...where are you all going?

You can come back now, Miss Rose!

Until tomorrow, Mr. Briar.

How was hanging with the enemy?
What?! I wasn't—

Relax! I'm just messing with you.
Heh. Right . . .

How were the mosquitoes?
Actually, I saw—

—never mind. We need to keep our eyes on the prize . . .

". . . I've got a feeling things are going to start looking up."

SQUAK
SQUAK

All right, everyone. Needles at the ready.

Very good, Tricia. Now, see if you can tighten the thread a bit.
Hey. You okay?

Ppbbt

Heh. Don't let your mom hear that attitude.
I don't think my feelings about quilt club will come as a surprise.

It's not so bad.

It's **quilting**, Lewis. It's pretty bad.

Ugh. Why can't I figure this ingredient thing out?
I keep thinking about what Blue said, hoping I'll pick up some clue. But I've got nothing.

I'm sorry, Al. I wish there was some way I could help.

That's it!

You **can** help, Lewis.
What's it?

You can become a Mapmaker too!
What?

It's perfect! If we're **both** Mapmakers, we can cover twice as much ground!
Cut the mapmaking time in half.
I don't think—

Blue **might** take a little convincing, but he'll come around. He has to! He will.
Al . . .

I don't **want** to be a Mapmaker!

I don't understand . . . we've been doing all this work . . .
You've been doing all this work. I'm just helping **you**.

But why, if you don't even care about it?

Because that's what we do—we do what **you** want to do!
That's not true . . .
Alidade, we never do what I want to do.

Okay, fine! What do you want to do? Stay in this town forever and **quilt**?!
Maybe!
Well, I won't do that!

Is there a **problem**, you two?
. . .

No.
There **was**. Not anymore.

We can both do what we want, Lewis.
Alidade . . .

Alone.

CRRK
SHHK
THUD

CRRK
SHHK
THUD
What—
—is that?

CRRK
Left alone for years and now I can't even get a good night's sleep!
SHHK
THUD

CRRK
SHHK
If it's you dreadful squirrels again, I will—
THUD

—oh.

GRRK

SHHK

OOF
THUD

And neither do I, apparently.

Alidade!
Leave me alone. I'm **trying**, okay?
I want to—wait.

What **are** you trying?
Hit the tree and see if the first ingredient falls out?

. . .

I'm doomed.

I've tried everything, but no matter what I do, I'm just . . . **lost**.

How can I ever be a Mapmaker if I'm always lost?

Do you ever wonder **why** you could see the entrance to the lodge?

How long did it sit **undisturbed**? And yet, **you** are the one who notices.

Everyone **else** in this Valley . . . they keep their eyes on the ground. Confident that's exactly where they belong.
But, Alidade . . .

. . . the lodge **only** reveals itself to those who are lost.

But then . . . how would a Mapmaker ever find it? Don't they always know where they're going?

Hah. No. **Clearly**, or maybe the Night Coats would not have **won**!

Mapmakers thrive because they are **comfortable** not knowing where they are going.
Everyone is lost, in a way.

Embracing the challenge—**that** is the key to being a Mapmaker.

It's why they do not run from their problems. Or **hide.**

Or hide from the problems of others.

I suppose I had forgotten that.

What?
Don't mind me. I'm just a silly old bird.
Now come on! There's work to be done still. Can't do it from the ground.

Your first instinct was to go for the **worms**. Why is that?
I don't know. They seemed . . .

. . . special.

Oh yes. And good food for the yellow-tailed ravens, too.

It's in the ravens' interest for the worms to thrive. That way, the ravens never have to look for a new home.

Hm.
First ingredient.

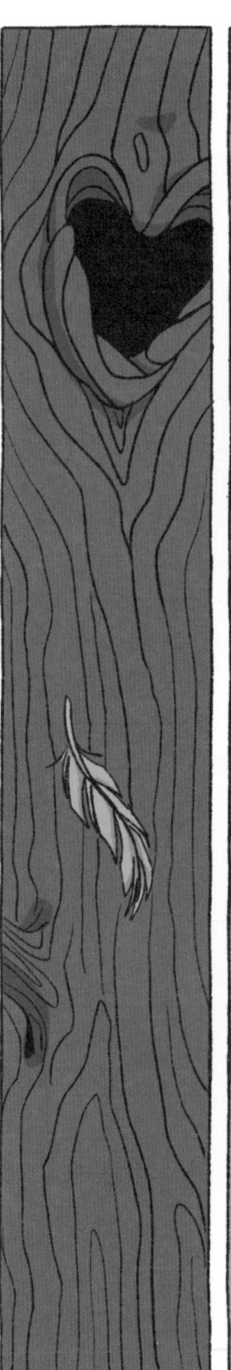

The first ingredient: my **quill**.

Very good!
Now the trickier part: why the feather and not the worms?

Because Mapmakers don't kill.
Yes, I believe we covered that . . .

At first, I saw all these individual parts and tried to pick one.

But really, each piece is part of the **whole**.
The tree isn't **broken**, it's a home for the worms.

The worms provide for the ravens.
Who in turn protect the nest.

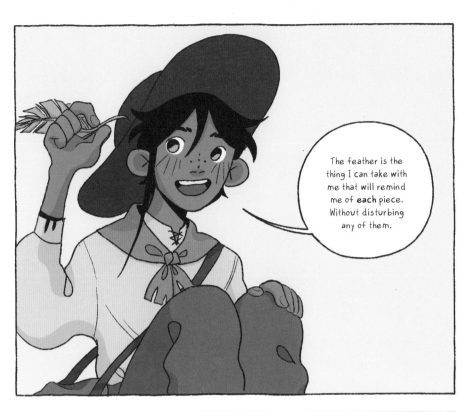

The feather is the thing I can take with me that will remind me of **each** piece. Without disturbing any of them.

Well done, Alidade Rose.

Thanks, Blue.

That—right there, do you feel that?
Feel what?
That **spark** of energy inside you!

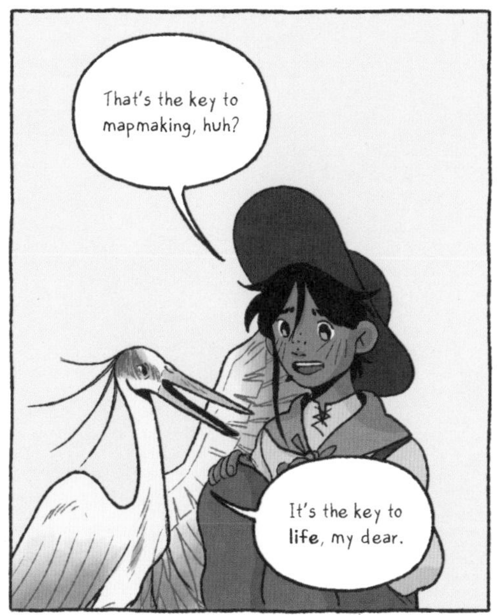
That's the key to mapmaking, huh?
It's the key to **life**, my dear.

So! You have your quill. A piece of the Valley itself will be captured in your every stroke.
Now comes the hard part.

That wasn't the hard part?
Not even close!

Now . . . we have to teach you how to **use** it.

Ingredients
"You would be surprised what you can find . . .
". . . when you know what to look for."

"What might seem mundane to the natural eye . . .

". . . can help create wonders."

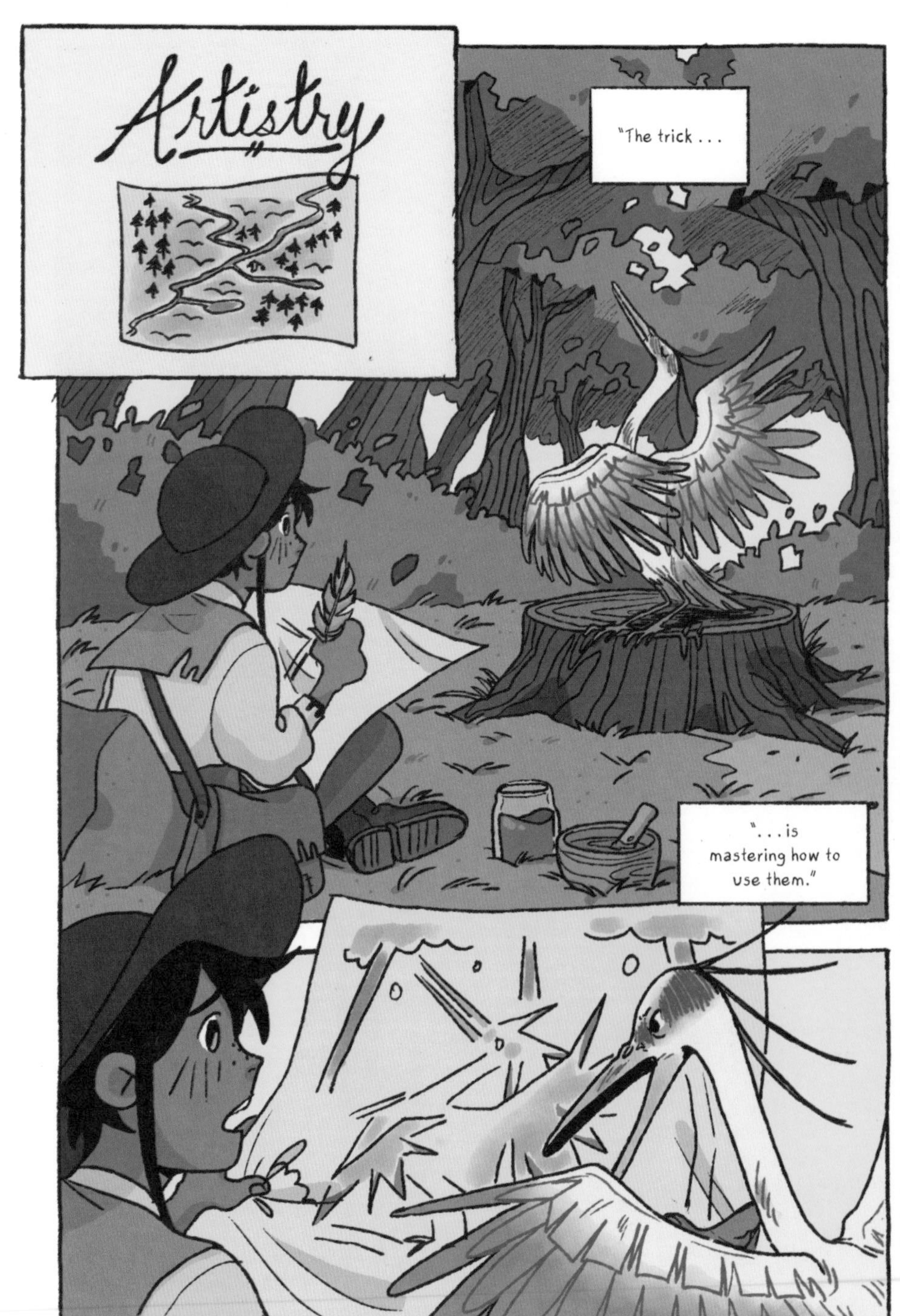
Artistry
"The trick . . .
". . . is mastering how to use them."

"Others have walked this same path. May they be your guide . . .

". . . and inspiration."

Accuracy
"But in the end, it is up to the Mapmaker to find their way.
"It is hard work, no doubt."

"But it is done so we might expand our horizons . . .
". . . and help others do the same."

All right, time for the compass rose. The final piece.

As soon as I finish this compass rose, you're going back to full strength.
Are you excited? Nervous?

Impatient.

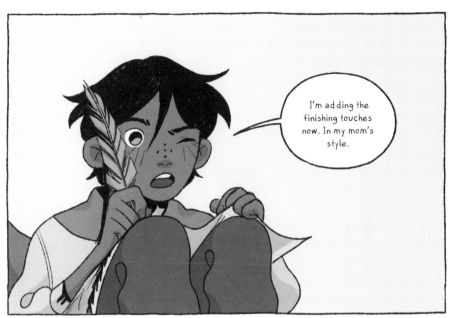

I'm adding the finishing touches now. In my mom's style.

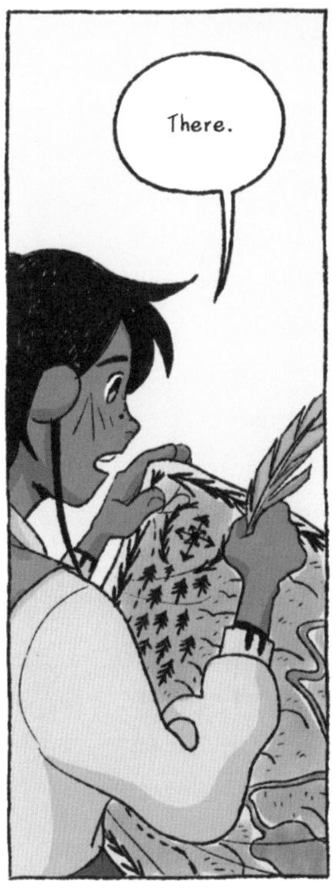

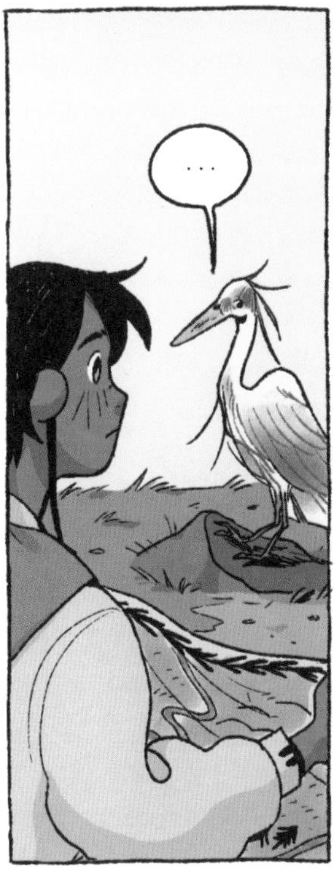

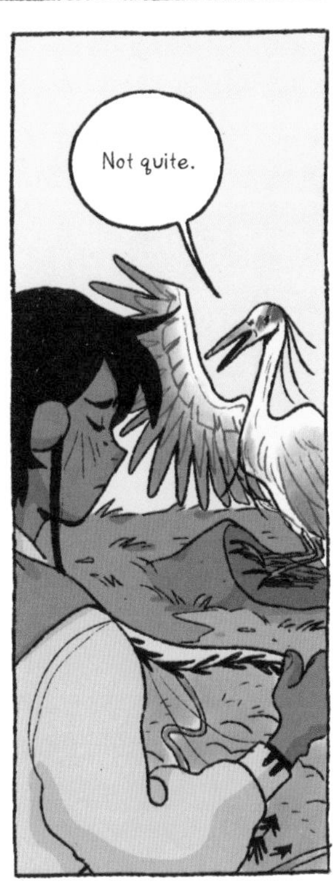

Uugghh.

And you're **sure** you're not at full strength?
All those jokes about my size and **now** you want to pretend it's normal?

Of **course** I'm not at full strength! Our map failed.

But . . . I did everything right. Like you taught me.

The map
is accurate now.
It . . . it **should**
work.

Of course
it doesn't! It's
this stupid
town!

This is the
only thing I've ever
asked of it, and it
can't even give me
that!
Aden

All it ever
does is **take**.

All alone, Mr. Briar?

I haven't seen you with Miss Rose as much these days.
She prefers it that way.

Ah. I'm sorry to hear that.
I hoped you'd rub off on her. Keep her from chasing the dangers that lie beyond town limits.

Dangers?

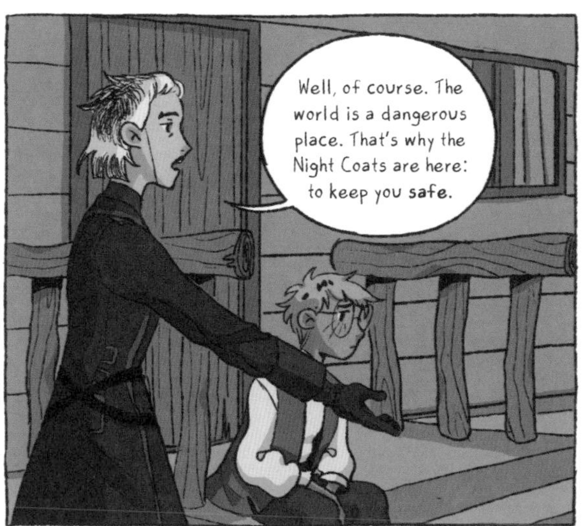
Well, of course. The world is a dangerous place. That's why the Night Coats are here: to keep you **safe**.

But I am sorry she's avoiding you. That's how she seems to treat **everyone** in Alden.

Not like **you**. You **know** everyone. And they all speak kindly of you.

You're a man of the people, Mr. Briar!

If you fall in line, I'm sure you won't be alone for long.

You all clean?

Yeah.
Good. Here, help me with the dishes.

What's wrong, hon?
Ma, what'd you and dad love so much about Alden? That makes you so . . . crazy about it?

Heh. Well, Alden is like most things in life—it is what you make of it.
And your father and I made it **ours**.

It can be rough around the edges, no doubt. But it's where we grew up and laughed and fell in love.
Really . . .

. . . it's us.

There's no perfect place in this world, Alidade. But if you're bold enough to set down roots . . .

. . . a place like Alden can grow into something special.

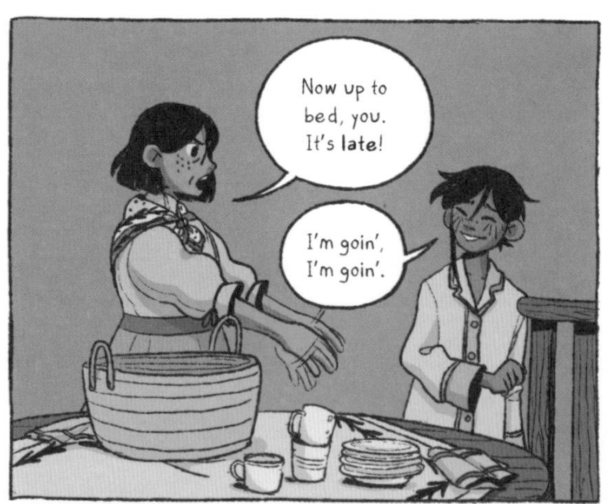
Now up to bed, you. It's **late**!
I'm goin', I'm goin'.

And, Alidade . . .
Whatever you're up to . . .

Please be **careful**.
I will!

Our beautiful girl and all her courage.

She must get that from **you**.

Alidade Rose, you come to the clay pit every day . . .

How are we **lost**?
I was looking for the mosquitoes again.

Ugh. I'm losing it, aren't I?

Well, if it is **mosquitoes** you were after . . .

. . . maybe we are not lost after all.

Hm. **These** mosquitoes are usually found near water and never in such great numbers. This is not typical behavior.

So . . . something in their environment is **atypical**?
Yes, good! But what?

Well . . .

. . . only one way to find out.

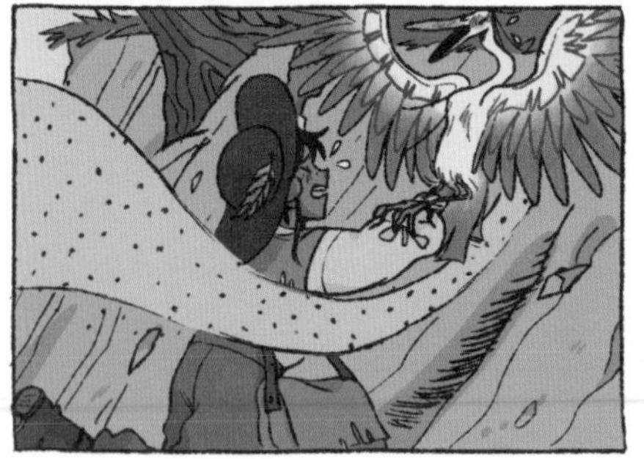

It appears we have arrived.
Bricks??

Never seen anything like **those** before.

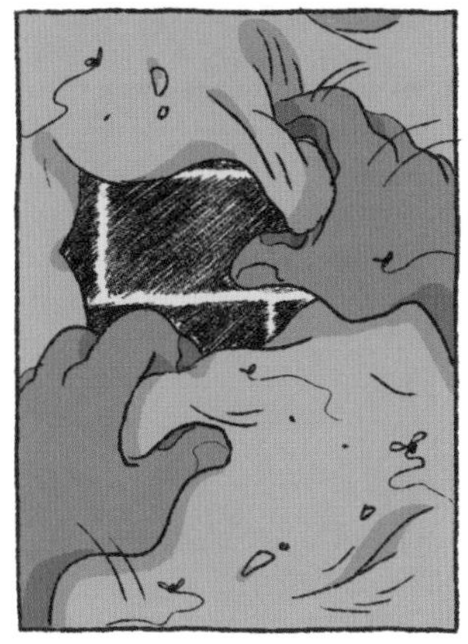

What is it?
Strange. I . . . do not know.

I don't remember seeing it on the map. It's like it doesn't exist.

Let's see what we can learn from a closer inspection.

Hnn!!
BLUE!!
Blue, wake up.
Please wake up!
Please.
DON'T MOVE!

Stay right where you are.
Hello, Miss Rose. What a surprise . . .

. . . always where you're **not** supposed to be.
Please . . . help?

A **Memri**?

What have you done?!

I thought you were just a **pest**. An annoyance.

But this— that **thing**—

Please.

NO!

You, Miss Rose, are no longer welcome here. By order of the Night Coats . . .

You are **banished**.
No! You— you can't—

You always wanted to see the outside world.

Now's your chance.

What **was** that, sir? The **thing** she was holding?

A remnant from a time gone by.

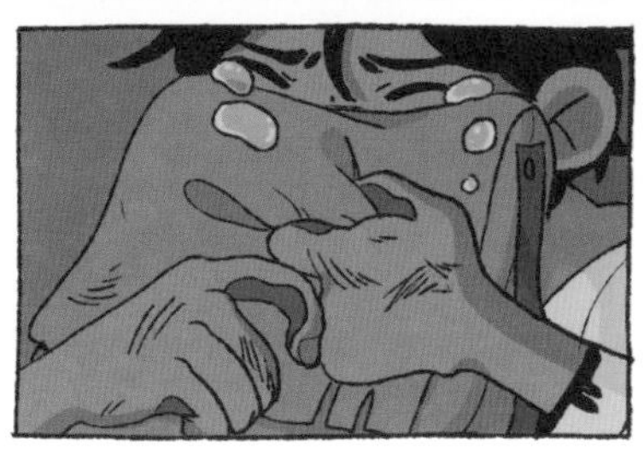

Excuse me. E-excuse me.

What—
what's going
on?
Oh, Lewis
dear, I'm so
sorry.

It's
your friend . . .
Alidade.

Alidade?!
Did you say
Alidade?
What
happened
to my girl?
Tell me.

Well,
uh . . .
The Night Coats
caught her past
town limits again.

She was **banished**.

Who told you this? **Where is she now**?!
I—I don't know! The Night Coats just reported what happened.

They—they said they warned us. Warned **her**.

I . . . I gotta go.
Lewis?

LEWIS! Where are you going?!

Alidade!!

ALIDADE!!

ALIDADE!

Hello?

Come on, Al.
Please be here.
Please.
Lewis?
!
Hey!

You're—you're still here.

Are you okay?
What **happened**?

Where . . .
where's Blue?

We found something. These dark bricks. They hurt Blue somehow and then the Constable . . .
The Constable destroyed the map and Blue's gone.

Alidade . . .
Alidade, I'm so **sorry**.
I failed him and now he's gone.

You shouldn't be here.
Eh. It should be a while before my folks realize I'm missing.

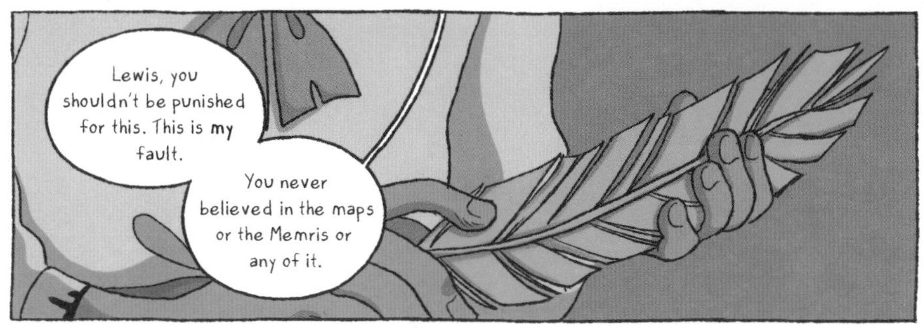
Lewis, you shouldn't be punished for this. This is **my** fault.
You never believed in the maps or the Memris or any of it.

Maybe, maybe not.

But, Alidade, I'll always believe in **you**.

I've wanted to leave Alden for so long.

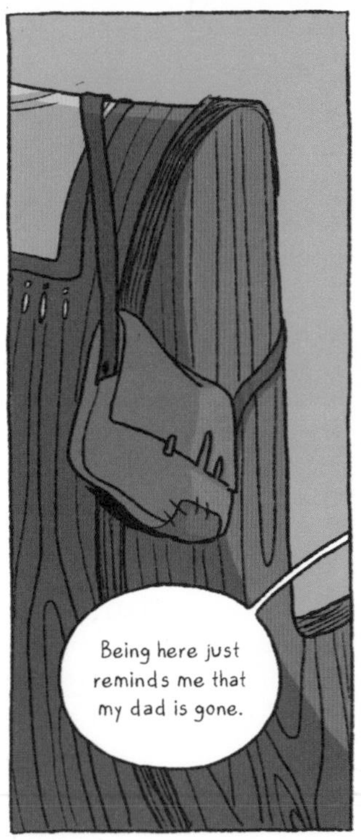
Being here just reminds me that my dad is gone.

I finally got the chance to go, but . . .
I realized, no matter **where** I go, he'll **always** be gone. Same with Blue.
I've lost them.

But I haven't lost **you**. If . . . you'll forgive me.

I'm sorry. For the way I acted. What I said.
It was nothing . . .

No, you were right!
Blue taught me that a Mapmaker must know how much they still have to learn.
And I still have a **lot** to learn about being a good friend.

Even if that means willingly going to quilt club.
It's not **that** bad.

What I don't get is, you kinda **stink** at quilting.
Oh, I **definitely** stink.
Then why is **that** the thing you want to do?

I don't know—it's not **about** that. It's just . . . I like being there. Seeing everyone together. It's nice.

Heh. That sounds like my Lewis.
Okay—if that's what you want to do, I'm with you.

You're wrong, you know.
What you said about your dad and Blue.

They're not gone no matter where you go . . .
You take them with you **wherever** you go.

But . . .
But what?
Why **should** we go?

The "Alden Way" might be keeping our heads down, but this is bigger than us—this is the **Valley**. Let's make a **new** way.

If anyone should leave, it's the Night Coats.

But I have no idea how we actually **do** that.

It's those dark bricks.

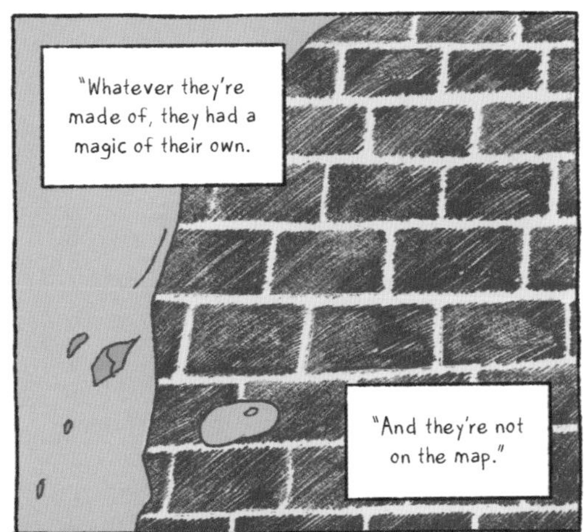
"Whatever they're made of, they had a magic of their own.
"And they're not on the map."

Whatever they are, they don't belong here. Like the Night Coats.
I just need more time to study them.

". . . the Constable is going to have eyes on that area nonstop.
"We'd need the whole town to distract them!"

Lucky for us, we have the one person who **could** rally the whole town.

. . .
Alidade, I don't think you're as popular as you think you are . . .

Not me! **You**! Lewis, you know **everyone**! Besides, your family alone is half the town.
Yeah, and when's the last time **they** noticed me?

It's your call. We do what **you** want to do. But I believe in you, Lewis. A lot of people do.
Okay . . .

". . . let's save
our Valley."

Be careful.
You too.

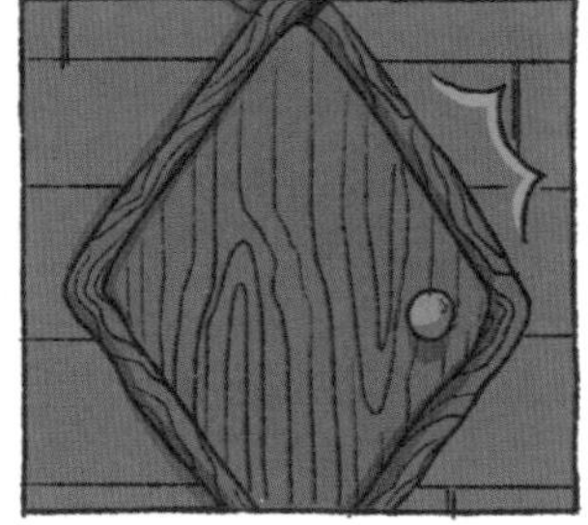

Okay, Lewis . . .

". . . you can do this."

Lewis Briar—
Mrs. Rose!
Did you find her?

I can only assume the reason you **ran off** was to find her. So—**did** you?

Yes. She's okay—we're working on it.
Working on it?

Can you organize an emergency quilt club meeting?
Lewis, everyone is hunkered down. They're worried about being banished from their homes!
Please . . .

Yes, of course . . .

". . . whatever Alidade needs."

I . . . I thought you said people were **hiding** out?
They are. They're just out **here** now.

PSST
MUTTER
That's a lot of people.
MURMUR
PSS
MURMUR

Alidade is out there somewhere, and if she's counting on the **quilt club**, I know she must be desperate.
Whaaat . . . Alidade totally loves the quilt club . . .

You're a good friend. Now stop overthinking and do what you've got to do.
Right.

. . . Can I have your attention? Please?
MUR MURR
WOAAH!
MUTTER
OOH!
PSS PSST
HMPH!
WAH!
HAH HAH!
MURR MUR
MUTTER

Um. Excuse me . . .
MURMUR
MUMBLE
MUTTER

PSS PSST
Uh. Hello?
MURMURR
MUMBLE
MUTTER

Is that Lewis?
Is who Lewis? Our Lewis?
HEY!
HMPH!
WAAAH!
MUMBLE
MURMUR

Dear, where is Lewis?
Oh no—we lost Lewis!

He's up there. Possibly making a fool of himself.

Excuse me,
everyone!

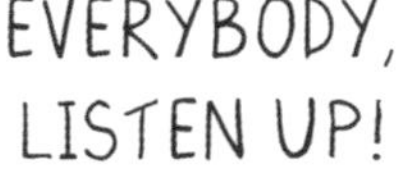
EVERYBODY,
LISTEN UP!

Thanks.

You're not here today for quilting, sorry. You all know by now—Alidade was banished.
So?!

What? I mean no ill will!
But we all saw the Constable **warn** Alidade. We're lucky she's the only one who got banished!

I see people pushed around in the pit every day. We all saw Mrs. Rose threatened in her own home.
I don't think any of us are lucky. Not while those Night Coats are here.

I'm with you, kid, but what do you want us to do? Cause a **ruckus**? That's not who we are.
Maybe not right now.

Mr. Carder—you stitched a square with a **trout**. Have you ever even fished before?

Uh. Not exactly. It's a family emblem!

Ms. Winchell—a **lily pad**? We ever get those in the pit?

"Lily" is a family name. Though I'm not sure why . . .

These things seem out of place, but . . . Alidade discovered something. Something we **used** to be.
A long time ago, a river ran through here.
I can only imagine what it was like. But if we look close, I think we can still see it.

To do that, we have to be like Alidade. We have to be curious and brave.
And for the **right reasons** . . . maybe break the rules a little bit.

Mr. Bradley, you say "that's not who we are," and the Night Coats would **agree** with you!

That's just how they want it. It's why they sent Alidade away.

But it's not too late—we can be more.

River, pit—
it doesn't really matter. Either way, this is our home.

I think it's time we pick our heads up and protect it.

WOO!
YEAH!
WHOOOOP!
WOOO HOOO!

Kid, how do you propose we actually **do** this?

Together.

Well?
No sign of her, sir. She's gone.

Should we send word up the chain . . .

. . . about our discovery?

Not yet. Not until I have all the facts. This isn't something to report **lightly**.
Sir!

In town . . .
You're going to want to see this.

Let's move.

Mr. Briar, I understand you're upset that your friend is gone, but it's no excuse for childish behavior.

Childish behavior? I saw this more as courageous defiance.

Heh. Seize him.

oof!

And what is that supposed to be?

Hnn—it's the flag of the Valley! Our flag.

Mr. Briar, when I said you were a man of the people, I had something far less rebellious in mind.

All right.
Time to figure
you out.

So there must be a way in.

kaff kaff
Yeah . . .

. . . this definitely wasn't on our map.

Oh,
Blue . . .
If you could
see this.

TMP
TMP
It can't be . . .
Miss Rose.

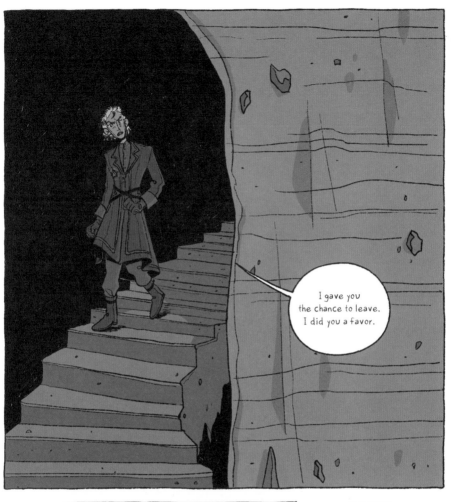

I gave you
the chance to leave.
I did you a favor.

Your next
punishment won't
be as kind.

You remind me of **myself** at your age, you know.
I tried to help you so you might find your **place**.

But I underestimated your reckless stupidity.

It didn't take long to realize your **friend** was merely a diversion.

I'm sorry he couldn't come through for you.

"He's being dealt with now."
Don't worry, Mr. Briar. The Constable will be back. And I imagine in an even worse mood.

She might kick **everybody** out of the Valley.

I highly doubt that.

?

We're not going anywhere.

You're making a mistake.

No, we're making a **choice**.

Now it's your turn.

What'll it be?

It's the river. Isn't it?

The Night Coats buried it down here for so long, everyone forgot it existed.
But the mosquitoes sensed it somehow.

And Blue . . . he remembered.

And what—you want to bring back the past? Erase progress for something you don't even remember?

You're lucky to grow up as you did! The Night Coats—this dam—kept you safe from the dangers the river invites!

How could you see Blue and believe any world would be better off **without** him?

You think the Memris care about humanity?

About our suffering? That your father died in front of your eyes?

Our lives are nothing but flickers to them! Gone in an **instant** and forgotten.
I—I don't believe you.

They don't care about **us**, Alidade! It's why the Night Coats exist.

Blue cared. For me. For Lewis.
For the Valley!

There is no "Valley"! Alden is **one** town of many, under one rule.

This—

—is a **fiction**.

And one **you** will no longer keep alive.
Alden!

Fttt

NO!
The world has changed.
Please . . .

It's time you accept that . . .

. . . just like everyone else.
Wait!

No no no

Alders

That's . . .
. . . all I had left of him.

They're not gone no matter where you go . . .
You take them with you **wherever** you go.

Now. On your feet.

Your fellow Aldeners will fall back in line once they see you've done the same.

Miss Rose . . .

We're **leaving**.

Alden

No.
What—

I'm not going anywhere.

What did you do?

Alden!

BLUE!
Alidade Rose . . .

. . . it's so good to see you.

And my **river**!
Hello, old friend.

Looks like you're ready to run out there where you belong.

Up you go, Alidade. We don't want to be underground when that happens.
Besides . . .

. . . I think you'll prefer the view from above.

There will be repercussions for this! We will come for you without mercy.
We've done it before.

The world will always be full of dangers, Constable Atwater. All we can do is face them bravely . . .

. . . alongside those we care for.

And we will do just that.

Wooohooo!

FWOOH

FWSH

CRSHH

Is—is that . . .
There was a river!

Look at it—it's beautiful!

Never seen anything like it.

Blue's map!

It's beautiful,
Blue.

What's
happening?!
Oh
no . . .

Must be the
map—we're
going down!

Oh boy.

I've got you,
I've got you!

I've—

—oof.

Lewis! You're all right!
Well, I . . . sort of had you.

And the town's okay?
Better than okay.
My map!

You saved it! Though that **gash** would explain why its magic did not hold.

I am sure we can fix that. Later.
Right now, there is something much more important at hand . . .

Constable!
Sir!

Are you all right, sir?
I'll be **fine.** What happened?

After you left, they ambushed us.
We were **outnumbered.** Had no choice but to fall back.
And how **far** back did you plan to go?

Home, sir.

Is it ready, Al?
Don't call attention to it—heaven forbid she realizes she's **quilting.**

It's not quilting **exactly.**

It counts! I'm counting it.

How's it coming along, Blue?

Quite nicely, I'd say.
A clever solution. One that feels . . . right.

There—done.

What do you think?

Tree with a Broken Heart.
Deer's prance
King Trout Lake

The Valley
Alden!
overlook
Lodge

It's beautiful, hon.
I love it so much.

I learned from the best.

Blue! You're **huge**!
More impressive, hm?

Oh yeah. You're definitely magic.

You have returned me to full strength, and more importantly, reminded me of something I had lost.
Well, hopefully the river stays put this time.

Not the **river**. You reminded me what makes you people worth all your trouble.

Your courage. Your thoughtfulness. Your **friendship**.

As long as there are people like you two, the world stands a chance.
And for that, I am truly grateful.

Blue . . . how did the Night Coats do it? Steal the river like that, I mean.

The Night Coats were responsible for the demise of the Memris long ago, but I had no idea they were capable of such dark magic.

But it gives me hope.

. . . how?
It means there are more Memris waiting to be reborn! More territories to be made new!

To do so, however, I shall need a Mapmaker.

And what about **this**? It—it won't come off . . .

Whatever you did, it worked.

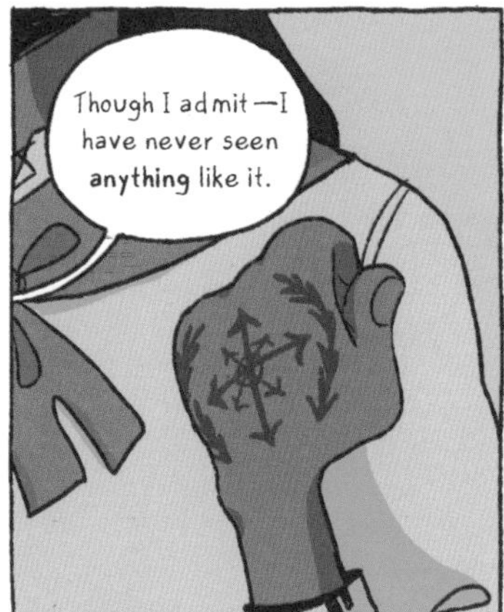
Though I admit—I have never seen **anything** like it.

This is one unknown we can **both** seek to understand. Agreed?
Agreed.

Do you **really** have to go? I'm sure those other Memris will be fine.
Ma, I'm a **Mapmaker** now! I have responsibilities, you know.
Blue will guide us. I promise.

You have my word.
I think I'll trust the person I've **always** trusted in that department.
Lewis?

I'll do my best, Mrs. Rose.
That's never failed us before.

I love you. Use that head of yours. I expect a full report on everything you learn.

Deal. Love you, too.

So, Blue . . .
what should we
expect to find
beyond that horizon,
anyway?

I have a
feeling the world's
a far different
place than the one
I remember.

Well,
whatever's
out there . . .

". . . we'll find it together."
To Be Continued

Autumn Squirrel
SHiNY FUR = HEALTHY SQUIRREL
SUUUPER SOFT!! softer than Blue!
A small rodent with a bushy tail and tufts on their ears. Named for their coat of fur that blends in with fall leaves. Ma thinks there are more of these critters in Alden than people.
Personality: Bold. Not scared of anything.
Food: Any kind of nuts or seeds they can find. (And if we're not careful, our lunch.)
THIS CARDINAL let ME get close! BLUE SAID THIS FEATHER WAS its gift to ME!
Black-Bellied Cardinal
A red bird with twin black markings on their face and chest. They can be found all year round, and with their constant singing, you won't miss them.
Personality: Lewis says they're "smug."
Call: A high-pitched and drawn-out stweee-pree-pree.

Me
And
dad
Dawnberry
looks
like
the
sunrise
LeAF
Round berries that grow on a small shrub and are ready for picking in the middle of summer.
Coloring: Reddish pink. Like a sunrise.
Taste: They have a sweet, floral taste. Dad would always wait until late summer to pick his so they tasted just a liiittle tart.
Twirl for something cool
Teal Lily
smells like a summer breeze
A wildflower found on the woodland floors. Inner and outer petals are different lengths and colors, but if you twirl them, they show a pretty teal ring. (What we didn't use for the map we gave to Lewis's sister. They're her favorite.)

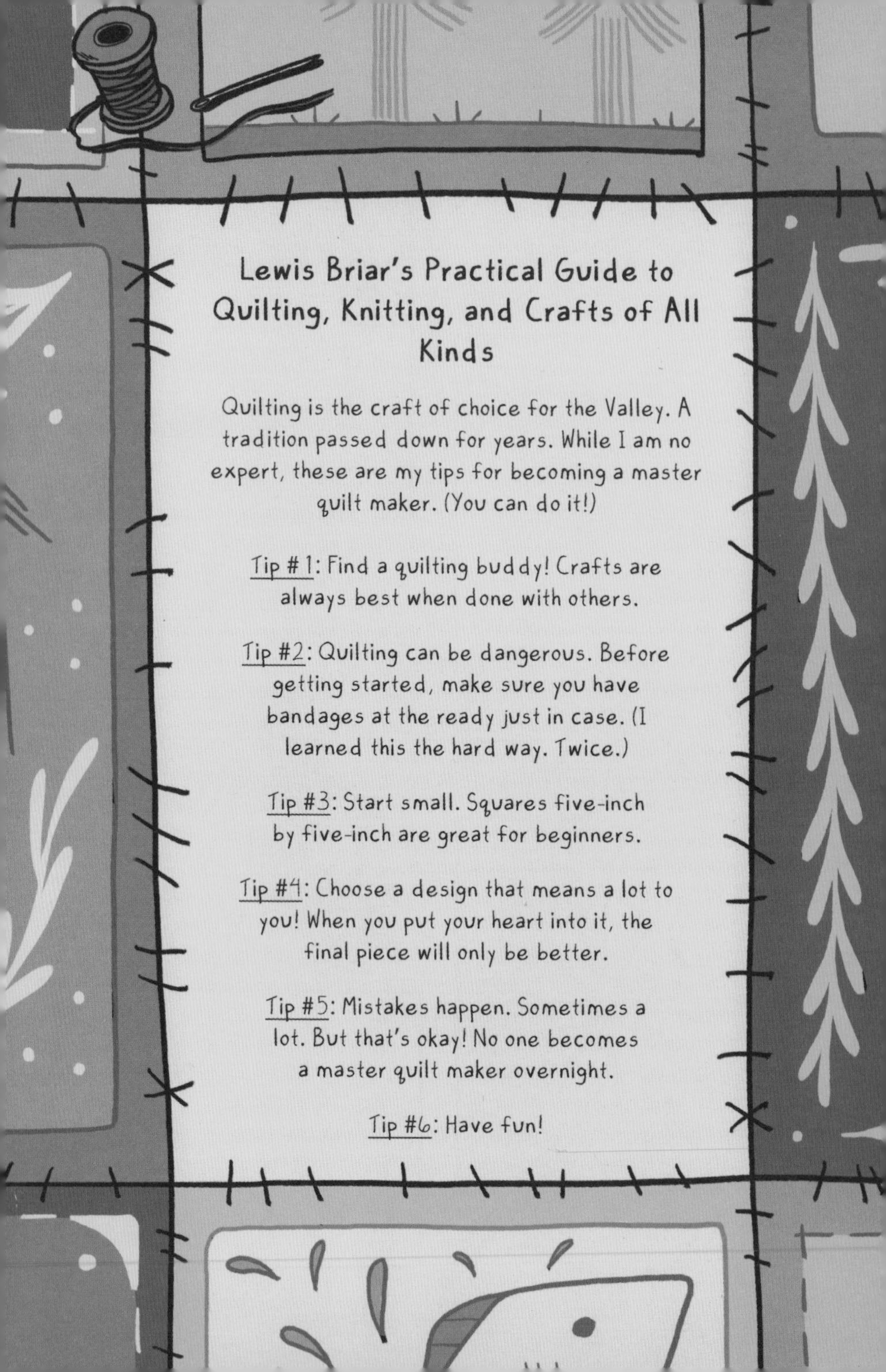

Lewis Briar's Practical Guide to Quilting, Knitting, and Crafts of All Kinds

Quilting is the craft of choice for the Valley. A tradition passed down for years. While I am no expert, these are my tips for becoming a master quilt maker. (You can do it!)

Tip #1: Find a quilting buddy! Crafts are always best when done with others.

Tip #2: Quilting can be dangerous. Before getting started, make sure you have bandages at the ready just in case. (I learned this the hard way. Twice.)

Tip #3: Start small. Squares five-inch by five-inch are great for beginners.

Tip #4: Choose a design that means a lot to you! When you put your heart into it, the final piece will only be better.

Tip #5: Mistakes happen. Sometimes a lot. But that's okay! No one becomes a master quilt maker overnight.

Tip #6: Have fun!

Drawing the Memri of the Valley
Quill at the ready, Mapmaker!
Today, we are going to learn how to draw a most noble and magical creature: **me**!
1
Every great illustration starts somewhere. When drawing **yours truly**, we begin with two ovals.
2
Once you add the **neck** and **wing**, a heron will start to take shape.
3
Now, be sure to keep an eye on **proportions**. I would hate to have wings too small or a tail too long.
4
Finally, add the details to your liking. Here you can showcase your **creativity**, a trait required by all Mapmakers.
Remember, it's okay if **your** Blue does not look exactly like this example. No two styles are alike, and that, my friend, is a good thing.

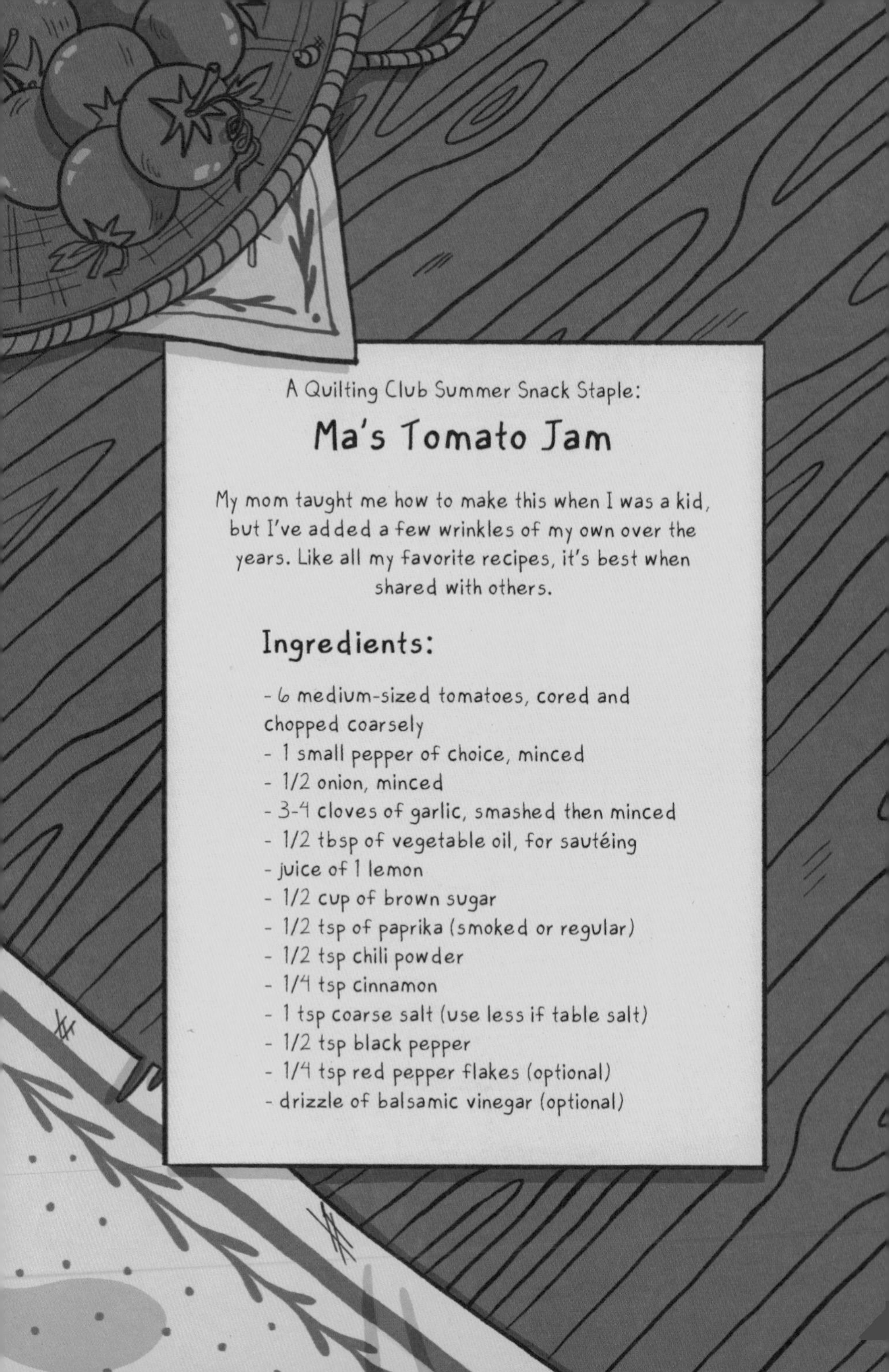

A Quilting Club Summer Snack Staple:

Ma's Tomato Jam

My mom taught me how to make this when I was a kid, but I've added a few wrinkles of my own over the years. Like all my favorite recipes, it's best when shared with others.

Ingredients:

- 6 medium-sized tomatoes, cored and chopped coarsely
- 1 small pepper of choice, minced
- 1/2 onion, minced
- 3-4 cloves of garlic, smashed then minced
- 1/2 tbsp of vegetable oil, for sautéing
- juice of 1 lemon
- 1/2 cup of brown sugar
- 1/2 tsp of paprika (smoked or regular)
- 1/2 tsp chili powder
- 1/4 tsp cinnamon
- 1 tsp coarse salt (use less if table salt)
- 1/2 tsp black pepper
- 1/4 tsp red pepper flakes (optional)
- drizzle of balsamic vinegar (optional)

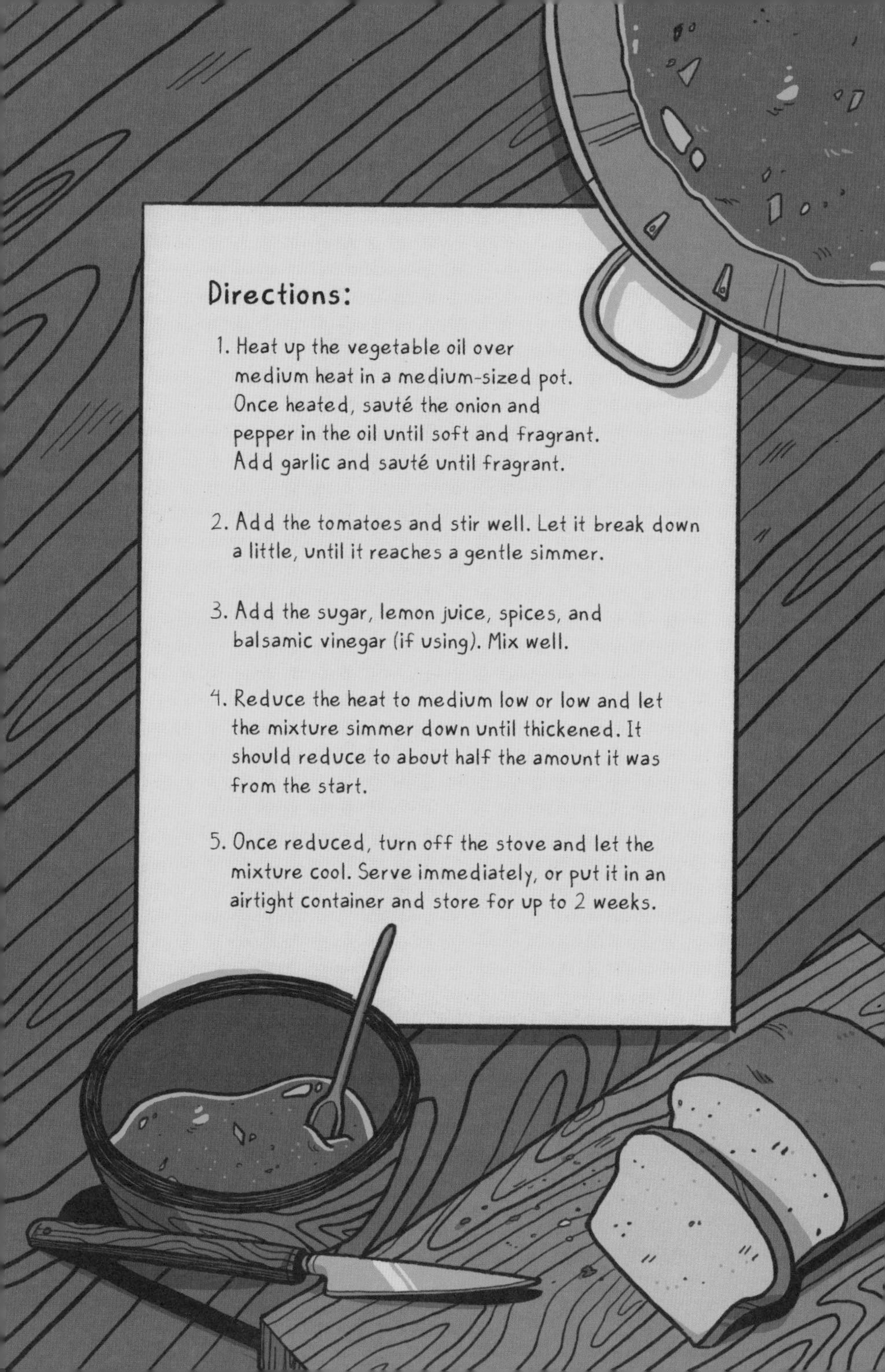

Directions:

1. Heat up the vegetable oil over medium heat in a medium-sized pot. Once heated, sauté the onion and pepper in the oil until soft and fragrant. Add garlic and sauté until fragrant.

2. Add the tomatoes and stir well. Let it break down a little, until it reaches a gentle simmer.

3. Add the sugar, lemon juice, spices, and balsamic vinegar (if using). Mix well.

4. Reduce the heat to medium low or low and let the mixture simmer down until thickened. It should reduce to about half the amount it was from the start.

5. Once reduced, turn off the stove and let the mixture cool. Serve immediately, or put it in an airtight container and store for up to 2 weeks.

Making of a Page

From concept to final

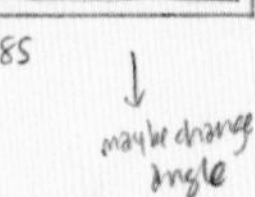

PG87

PAGE 86

Panel 1: Vertical panel stretching the whole page as the two kids climb up the tree. Alidade's a little bit higher than Lewis, taking the fastest (and more adventurous) route. She's got her head up, constantly searching. Meanwhile, Lewis has got his eyes on the yellow-tailed ravens, perched in the tree and fluttering about.

ALIDADE: Keep your eye out for something special.

Panel 2: The first of three equal stacked panels to the right of the vertical panel. Lewis has stopped mid-reach for a branch when he spots the gnarly looking yellow-tailed perched there and eying him suspiciously.

LEWIS: Uh–these yellow-tailed ravens look more...**hungry** than special.

RAVEN: SQWAK!

Panel 3: On Alidade as she leaps off both feet from one sturdy branch to a bigger one higher up. She's really going for it.

ALIDADE: They're **birds**. They're not going to **eat** you.

Panel 4: View from level with this new higher branch as Alidade pulls herself up, a soft yellow-green light shining on her face.

ALIDADE: But I think I found what they **do** eat...

*see the final art on page 86!

Final Designs

Alternate Color Palettes

Additional Character Designs

Younger Alidade and the Rose Family

The Briar Family

Constable Atwater and Night Coats Ada and Tace

When designing Alidade and Lewis, there were only a few key elements that Cam wanted to be included, such as Alidade's hat and scarf, as well as Lewis's glasses and short-cropped hair, but the rest was up to me. My intent with their designs was to have them play off of each other in a way that would make the other stand out even more, and for me, a good place to always start is understanding their personalities: Alidade, who is bold and always ready for adventure; Lewis, who is careful and a kindhearted, community-oriented kid.

In addition to Alidade and Lewis, I decided to create final designs for their respective families as well so that the two kids could feel more integrated into the world around them. Alidade's scarf is one of her distinctive features, so I gave her family their signature green tones to jump off of. Lewis comes from a big family with big personalities so I worked to figure out how to make each member individualized, as well as cohesive as a whole so that they really felt like they belonged together.

The Night Coats, on the other hand, served to create a contrast to the world where Alidade and Lewis come from. They're outsiders and not from the Valley, not really understanding the place and its true worth. The Night Coats' rigid and neutral-colored designs serve to separate them from the Valley folk, whose natural and humble designs tie them to the land.

Lodge Exterior Sketches

Early Valley Lodge Designs

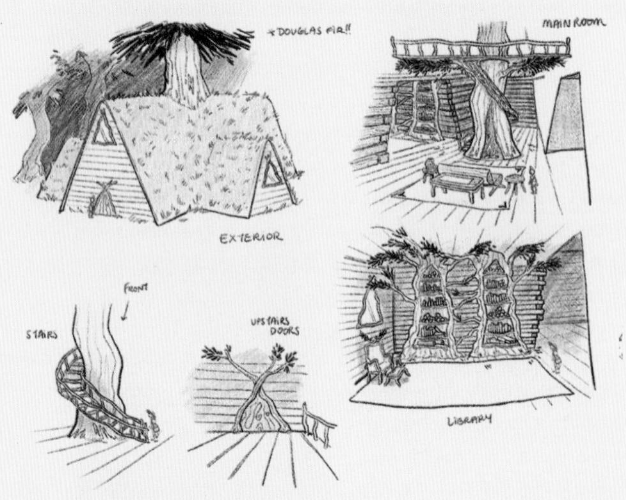

Valley Lodge Rough Layout

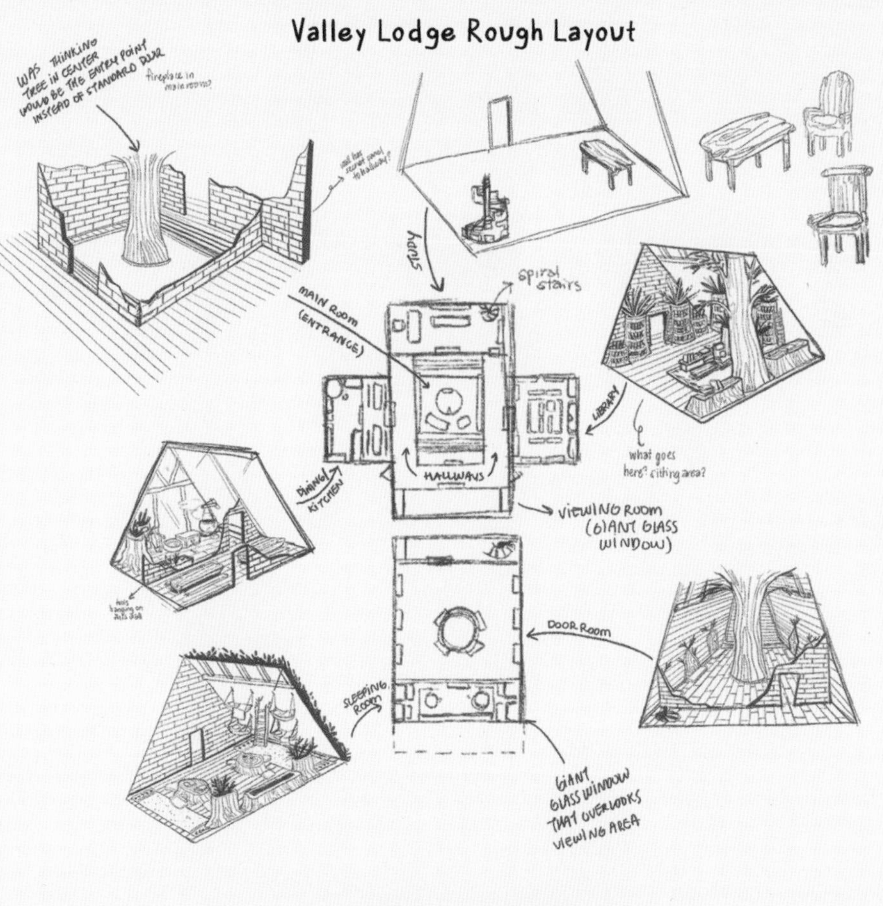

Designing the Valley Lodge was the most difficult task when it came to creating this world. There were certain points of inspiration that Cam provided: Frank Lloyd Wright's Cedar Rock, Wayfarers Chapel in California, and the idea that this lodge is integrated with its surroundings. Going off the idea that the doorway for this lodge is in a tree, I decided to keep that tree as the central point of the lodge. Since the lodge is a place for Mapmakers to travel through and take a rest, I also thought about what the coolest forest cabin would look like and what would be essential to travelers. To me, that's lots of high spaces, slanted ceilings, a big community kitchen area, and wide open windows to see all the greenery outside!

Note from the Writer

I have a terrible sense of direction. I get turned around easily, don't risk driving without a GPS, and lose my way on the most routine travels. This is true even when writing.

I can be deep into a script and realize I'm not sure how to get to the other side. Influences and inspirations change. What seemed like a perfect ending suddenly seems out of place.

In those moments during the writing of *Mapmakers and the Lost Magic*, I turned to the things that give me a feeling of home: My favorite places in Northeast Ohio, Southern California, and New England. The books and comics I devoured as a kid. Family and friends.

I knew that if I could somehow capture those feelings in Alidade's story, even just a tiny bit, I could guide her on this journey. After all, despite my frequent detours and wrong turns, I always find my way home.

Note from the Artist

When I read the first draft of this script, I thought it would tell a simple adventure story about a young girl who wanted to seek out and understand the secrets of the land she comes from. In a sense, it does, but while I worked on it, it became so much more to me.

The time I worked on this book has harbored some of the biggest changes in my life, and Alidade and her story have become an anchor point for me to hold on to. During the year and a half that I worked on this book, I came to the slow realization that Alidade reminds me of myself as a child, frustrated at the world and yearning to leave home to see what the world has in store, and encapsulates everything I wished I was when I was younger: brave, determined, and honest with herself.

Alidade's journey as a character has been such a special one for me because the lessons she learns and realizations she makes reminded me of those I had to come to understand when I was growing up and even to this day. Just like Alidade, I learned how important and powerful the community you come from or surround yourself with is, that there is so much that is better off done together, with the people you love and trust. And, along with Alidade, I have grown over the course of this book, further learning and understanding the traits that I had admired in her within myself.

Going into the design for Alidade, I knew that I wanted her to be a character I wished to see when I was a kid. Someone who's not defined by her appearance alone, but rather by the way she's able to act so unabashedly like herself. As Alidade and only Alidade. And now, as this book goes out into the hands of countless kids in the world, I hope she can inspire you the way she has inspired me. To me, Alidade's story is a representation that for every person who feels lost, there is a community—a beacon of light, a compass rose—ready to help guide you home.

Acknowledgments

While writing may be a solitary act, there are countless people in my corner who make it possible.

I can never give enough thanks to my entire family—the Chittocks, Njoyas, and Taylors—for their love and belief in me.

I would not even be a writer without the encouragement and patience of teachers like Michael Stahl, Lee Fallon, and Mildred Lewis.

During the development process, I received invaluable enthusiasm and feedback from Sierra Hahn, David Petersen, and Doug Smit. I was also lucky enough to join an incredible school community that supported me (and kept me sane) each and every day.

The wonderful folks at Random House Graphic believed in us from the beginning and worked tirelessly on behalf of this book. I need to specially thank our designer, Patrick Crotty, and our editor, Whitney Leopard. They deserve all the credit.

Comics is an artist's medium, and I'm so grateful to work with truly one of the best. Amanda's thoughtfulness, creativity, and collaboration made this story, and the experience of telling it, far better than I ever could have imagined.

Finally, no matter what stage of the writing process I was in, I got to end each day by sharing what I wrote with my best friend and favorite reader. Whatever I was working on, talking story with my wife, Tay, ensured I never felt like I was writing alone.

—Cameron

The journey of making a full graphic novel is never an easy one, especially the first time.

I'd like to thank our amazing editor, Whitney, and designer, Patrick, for all the patience, understanding, and words of encouragement they've given along the way. I really couldn't have asked for a greater team to help guide the telling and the look of this book in the right direction. I'd also like to extend this thanks to everyone at Random House Graphic and those involved with making this book what it was, for believing in this tale and everything we hoped to accomplish with it.

Going into this process for the first time was definitely intimidating, but working with a writer as thoughtful, creative, and supportive as Cam made it so much more possible to achieve what I thought I couldn't do. Every time he crafted new words or shared new ideas, I was only inspired more and more by this world. Thank you for believing in me and trusting me to assist with bringing your vision to life. To say I'm honored in helping it become a reality is a huge understatement.

My unending gratitude goes to Ryan Sands, for allowing me to assist with Youth in Decline as a wee baby college student who didn't know exactly what they wanted to do yet. Your unending love for comics and their creators inspired me, as well as helped me realize what it was I wanted to do and gave me the space to start creating stories I wanted to tell.

I'd like to thank my professors from college—Allan, Shadra, and Aya—for your belief in me as an artist. Without your support and motivation to challenge myself, I wouldn't be in the position I am today.

Finally, I'd like to thank all my loved ones. First and foremost, my mom and dad; my sister, Isabelle; as well as the rest of my family. You helped me grow up in an environment of love and encouragement, believing in me and what I do every single day. Without your endless support, I wouldn't be where I am right now and I couldn't express the gratitude and love I feel for you through words alone. To Sara, Victoria, Abelle, Angie, Emily (and Andy too!), Megan, Steph, Sara, Taylor, Sophie, and Emily: your friendship throughout the years has been and will always be irreplaceable. To be able to share this book with you isn't nearly enough thanks for all the support and love you've given me.

You are all my Alden. You are all my home.

The art for this book was created on the occupied lands of the Piscataway, Ohlone, and Onondaga (Seneca) peoples.

—Amanda

Cameron Chittock is a writer from Northeast Ohio. He grew up surrounded by siblings, wildlife, and comics of all kinds. Cameron's writing is possible thanks to patient teachers, encouraging friends, and a supportive family. His favorite stories are those of heroes and friendship. Cameron previously edited comics, including titles such as the Eisner Award-nominated graphic novel *New World*, *Mech Cadet Yu*, and *Jim Henson's The Power of the Dark Crystal*. He now lives in New England and works in education. When he's not writing, he enjoys coaching basketball, reading giant fantasy books, and sitting by the pond with his family. *Mapmakers and the Lost Magic* is his debut graphic novel.

cameronwtchittock.com
@CameronChittock

Amanda Castillo is a comic artist, illustrator, and storyteller, born and raised in the Bay Area in California. Having grown up inspired by piles of manga, games about friendship and adventure, and the endless wonders of the California outdoors, Amanda went on to study illustration to hone a skill set to tell warm and heartfelt stories that could be enjoyed and remembered by someone like you! After getting into the comics world through working with Youth in Decline, Amanda has since contributed to publishers such as BOOM! Studios, Lion Forge, and now Random House Graphic. In addition to making comics, Amanda has shown work in galleries domestically and helped judge annual comics awards. When not making comics, Amanda enjoys spending time with friends and loved ones, making warm and hearty meals, learning to tend to plants, and taking in the lovely moments the world has to offer. *Mapmakers and the Lost Magic* is their debut graphic novel.

amanda-castillo.com
@mandallin

Never seen that before!
Ooh! What's that over there?!
At this rate, we'll never reach . . .
. . . where are we going exactly?
Over root and stone, through snow and sleet, to the top of the great mountain!
Ooh, look! A way home!

MAPMAKERS

The adventure continues in 2023!